GOLDILOCKS
and THE THREE BEARS

Retold and illustrated by
JAMES MARSHALL

SCHOLASTIC INC.
New York Toronto London Auckland Sydney

For Trevor Brandon Johnson

Previously published in Canada by Fitzhenry & Whiteside Limited, Toronto.

ISBN 0-590-44992-3

24 23   1 2/0

Printed in the U.S.A.   08

First Scholastic printing, September 1991

Once there was
a little girl called Goldilocks.
"What a sweet child,"
said someone new in town.
"That's what *you* think,"
said a neighbor.

One morning Goldilocks's mother
sent her to buy muffins in the next village.
"You must promise *not* to take the shortcut
through the forest," she said.
"I've heard that bears live there."
"I promise," said Goldilocks.
But to tell the truth Goldilocks
was one of those naughty little girls
who do *exactly* as they please.

Meanwhile in a clearing
deeper inside the forest,
in a charming house all their own,
a family of brown bears
was sitting down to breakfast.

"Patooie!" cried big old Papa Bear.
"This porridge is scalding!
  I've burned my tongue!"
"I'm dying!" cried Baby Bear.
"Now really," said Mama Bear,
  who was of medium size.
"That's quite enough."

"I know," said Papa Bear.
"Why don't we go for a spin
while the porridge is cooling?"
"Excellent," said Mama Bear.
So they got on their rusty old bicycle
and off they went.

A few minutes later
Goldilocks arrived
at the bears' house.
She walked right in
without *even* bothering to knock.
On the dining room table
were three inviting bowls
of porridge.
"I don't mind if I do,"
said Goldilocks,
helping herself
to the biggest bowl.

But the porridge in the biggest bowl was much too hot.
"Patooie!" cried Goldilocks.
And she spat it out.
Next she tasted the porridge in the medium-sized bowl.
But that porridge was much too cold.

Then Goldilocks tasted the porridge in the little bowl, and it was *just right*—neither too hot nor too cold.

In fact she liked it so much
that she gobbled it all up.

Feeling full and satisfied Goldilocks thought
it would be great fun to have a look around.
Right away she noticed
a lot of coarse brown fur everywhere.
"They must have kitties," she said.

In the parlor there were three chairs.
"I don't mind if I do," she said,
climbing into the biggest one.
But the biggest chair was much too hard,
and she just couldn't get comfortable.

Next she sat in
the medium-sized chair.
But that chair was much too soft.
(And she thought she might *never* get out of it.)

Then Goldilocks sat in the little chair,
and that was *just right*—
neither too hard nor too soft.
In fact she liked it so much
that she rocked and rocked—
until the chair fell completely to pieces!

Now, all that rocking left
Goldilocks quite tuckered out.
"I could take a little snooze,"
she said.
So she went to look
for a comfy place to nap.
Upstairs were three beds.
"I don't mind if I do," said Goldilocks.
And she got into the biggest one.
But the head of the biggest bed
was much too high.

Next she tried the medium-sized bed.
But the head of that bed was much too low.
Then Goldilocks tried the little bed, and it was *just right*.
Soon she was all nice and cozy and sound asleep.
She did not hear the bears come home.

The three bears were mighty hungry.
But when they went in for breakfast,
they could scarcely believe
their eyes!
"Somebody has been in
my porridge!" said Papa Bear.
"Somebody has been in
my porridge!" said Mama Bear.
"Somebody has been
in my porridge,"
said Baby Bear.
"And eaten it all up!"

The three bears went upstairs on tiptoe
(not knowing what they would discover).
At first everything seemed fine.
But then Papa Bear lay down on his
big brass bed.
"Somebody has been lying
in my bed!" he cried.
And he was not amused.

"Egads!" cried Mama Bear.
"Somebody has been lying
  in *my* bed!"
"Look!" cried Baby Bear.
"Somebody has been lying in my bed.
  And she's still there!"

"Now see here!" roared Papa Bear.
Goldilocks woke up with a start.
And her eyes nearly popped out of her head.
But before the bears could demand
a proper explanation, Goldilocks was out of bed,

out the window, and on her way home.
"Who *was* that little girl?" asked Baby Bear.
"I have no idea," said Mama Bear.
"But I hope we never see her again."

And they never did.